EA   ARY

D0363152

This MAMMOTH belongs to

_____

_____

_____

for Finny and Alice and
Evan and Min,
(because they never got to see any
foxes when they
came to
stay).

Whistling in the Woods

Selina Young.

MAMMOTH

EAST SUSSEX						
V	BFS	INV No.	7216301			
SHELF MARK						
COPY No.						
B R N						
DATE		LOC	LOC	LOC	LOC	LOC	LOC
COUNTY LIBRARY						

H<small>ERE ARE THE WOODS</small>, and they're dark and they're grim.

Here is the path, and it's long and it's thin.

Here are the trees that line the path,
so tall they touch the sky.
And here in the woods, all dark and grim,
are fox cubs enough to make ten.

Sneaking and creeping and chittering and chattering,
out from the woods the fox cubs come.
First One then Two, but Three is late.

Four and Five arrive and they wait,
till at last comes Three, skipping along.

Then the rest follow: Six, Seven and Eight,
with Nine who's quite shy and Ten who is brave.
And slowly, but surely, they
all get home safe.

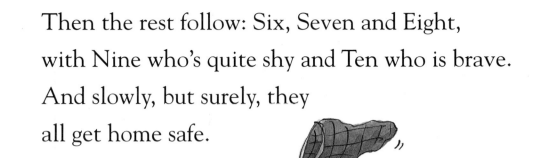

At home in their den Mother Fox makes the tea.
The tatties and gravy are bubbling in the pot,
when in come those fox cubs, hungry as can be.

They wash their front paws (*twenty in all*).
Then they hear their mother call:
"Tea's on the table."

After tea Mother Fox shoos them out to play.
She wipes all ten noses and warns them
"Be careful cubs. Don't stray."

All at once, Eight pricks up his ears,

a strange snuffling he hears.

Whatever can it be?

Suddenly, out from the bushes comes something in red,
sniffling and snuffling like you wouldn't believe.
Eight creeps towards it, Ten spies it too,
and he tugs at its vest and asks, "What are you?"

"I'm Rosy and I'm lost," the red thing replies.
"Have you never seen a girl all lost and alone
who can't find her way home?"
The little cubs shake their heads.
"Well, no. We never have," they say.

The fox cubs start creeping and tiptoeing in,
and curiously they circle the snuffling thing.
And as they get braver and bolder,
they push and they pull and they pinch and they prod.

"Oh stop!" Rosy cries. "I want to go home."
And she sobs and she sniffs and she
stamps her red shoe.

So
the little cubs
think and they hum
and they hah, and they put
their ten heads together. While
they dream up ideas to get Rosy home,
the daylight is ending and the moon is
arriving. In the cool of the evening
the clouds start to gather. The
trees are swaying and the
wind whistles softly
through the grass.
Whistle .....
whistle ....
whistle!

WHISTLE! That's what they'll do.
The fox cubs all clap and Rosy laughs,
for they've thought how she can be found.

So ten paws and one little hand each pick a lush
blade of grass. Three goes first and shows them all how
to use it to whistle out loud.
Hold it up to your snout.
Take a deep breath.
And gently blow on the grass.
Like sooooooooo!

WHЄEEE@*!eeeeT!!!!!!

Eleven blaring whistles ring out through the trees.
They do it again and again. Oooh it's fun!

They whistle and whistle for help.

Soon they hear the soft thud of footsteps on pine needles,
and out from the trees steps Rosy's dad.

He hugs and kisses her and says how he's missed her.

Then Rosy remembers her friends.

But when she turns round, there's not one to be found.

She calls them in vain, and tries to explain to her dad,
but he doesn't reply. He just hushes and shushes
and whisks her back home.

All warm in the kitchen while Mum gets
the tea, Rosy tells them about
her adventure.
"I was lost and alone when
out from the trees came
ten friendly fox cubs.
They helped me find Dad.

ROSY

WIPE
AWAYS

They taught me to *whistle*."
Mum and Dad nod their heads and agree,
but they don't really believe her
(they're grown up
you see).

But later that night, when the house is in darkness,
the foxcubs creep into Rosy's garden
to see if she's safe.

Rose Cottage

They're chattering and whistling, but Rosy's not listening.
She's snuggled down deep and fast asleep.

She'll never go off and get lost again,
even if she hears those friendly foxcubs
WHISTLING IN THE WOODS.

First published in Great Britain 1994
by William Heinemann Ltd
Published 1995 by Mammoth
an imprint of Reed Consumer Books Ltd
Michelin House, 81 Fulham Road, London SW3 6RB
and Auckland, Melbourne, Singapore and Toronto

Copyright © Selina Young 1994
The right of Selina Young to be identified as
author and illustrator of this work has
been asserted by her in accordance with the
Copyright, Designs and Patents Act 1988

ISBN 0 7497 2508 7

A CIP catalogue record for this title
is available from the British Library

Produced by Mandarin Offset
Printed and bound in Hong Kong

This paperback is sold subject to the condition
that it shall not, by way of trade or otherwise,
be lent, resold, hired out, or otherwise circulated
without the publisher's prior consent in any form
of binding or cover other than that in which
it is published and without a similar condition
including this condition being imposed
on the subsequent purchaser.